PETE'S CHICKEN

Harriet Ziefert

pictures by **Laura Rader**

Tambourine Books New York

The text type is Century Schoolbook

Printed in Singapore

Library of Congress Cataloging in Publication Data

Ziefert, Harriet. Pete's Chicken/by Harriet Ziefert; illustrated by Laura Rader.
1st ed. p. cm. Summary: Pete draws a special chicken in school, but the
other kids laugh and the teacher doesn't pin it on the bulletin board.
[1. Drawing—Fiction. 2. Individuality—Fiction.] I. Rader, Laura,
ill. II. Title. PZ7.Z487Pf 1994 [E]—dc20 93-37314 CIP AC
ISBN 0-688-13256-1 (TR). — ISBN 0-688-13257-X (LE)
1 3 5 7 9 10 8 6 4 2
First edition

For my children, James, Jon, and Allison   H.M.Z.

For Scott   L.R.

I'm me.
One of a kind.

In all the world you won't find anyone who is exactly like me.

Nobody else looks
like me. Not Sam.
Not Henry.
Not Binny.
Not Joe.
Not anyone.

I have a round face...

black eyes...

a big nose...

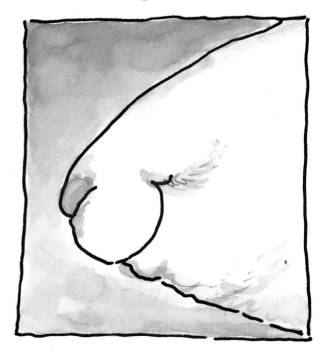

crooked ears…

and a nice smile.
That's me!

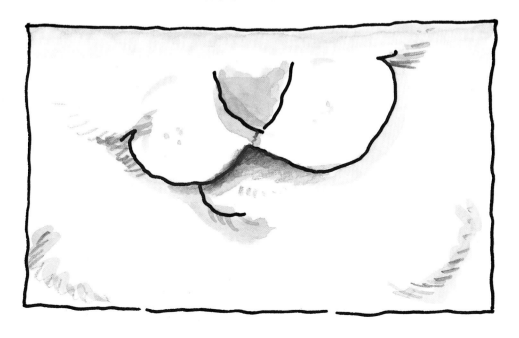

I do things
my own special way—
not like anyone else.

I play hard.

I build high.

I run crooked.

I go to Wildwood School.
One day the art teacher said,
"Today we will all draw chickens."

I turned over my crayon box and
spilled out all the colors.
First I drew with the black crayon.
I made a chicken shape.

I colored and colored until I used
all the colors of the rainbow.
My chicken was finished.
I smiled at him. I liked him.

The art teacher held up my picture.
"Let's all look at Pete's chicken," she said.
"It has an orange head, blue wings, red thighs,
    purple feet, a yellow body, and a green tail."

Everyone laughed.

Henry said, "That's some weird chicken!"
And Binny whispered, "Pete made a turkey...
Pete made a turkey... Pete made a turkey."

The teacher hung six chickens on the bulletin board. She put the others on a pile on the desk.

It made me sad
to leave my chicken
on top of a desk,
so I took mine home.

My mom wanted a kiss,
but I didn't feel like it.

I said, "Look at my chicken.
I drew it in art."

Mom said, "It's a beautiful chicken."

I said, "Everyone at school made
fun of it. Binny said I made a turkey."

And I went to my room.

I lay down on my bed. I wanted to be alone. I thought about what happened in school. Finally, I said to myself, "I'm me. Nobody else looks like me. Not Sam. Not Henry. Not Binny. Not anyone. And nobody makes chickens like me...not anyone!"

I picked up my chicken—
with its orange head, blue wings,
red thighs, purple feet,
yellow body, and green tail.

I ran to my mom and said,

"Let's hang this picture.
It's a beautiful chicken!"